CHICAGO BEARS

BY JOSH ANDERSON

Stride
An Imprint of The Child's World®
childsworld.com

The Child's World®
childsworld.com

Published by The Child's World®
800-599-READ • www.childsworld.com

Photography Credits
Cover: © Jonathan Daniel / Staff / Getty Images; page 1: © Africa Studio / Shutterstock; page 3: © Christian Petersen / Staff / Getty Images; page 5: © Rey Del Rio / Stringer / Getty Images; page 6: © Handout / Getty Images; page 9: © Jamie Squire / Staff / Getty Images; page 10: © Jamie Squire / Staff / Getty Images; page 11: © stevezmina1 / Getty Images; page 12: © Jonathan Daniel / Staff / Getty Images; page 12: © James Gilbert / Stringer / Getty Images; page 13: © Jonathan Daniel / Staff / Getty Images; page 13: © Jonathan Daniel / Staff / Getty Images; page 14: © Jonathan Daniel / Staff / Getty Images; page 15: © David Banks / Stringer / Getty Images; page 16: © TSN/Icon SMI / Newscom; page 16: © Al Golub/ZUMA Press / Newscom; page 17: © Jonathan Daniel / Stringer / Getty Images; page 17: © Jonathan Daniel / Staff / Getty Images; page 18: © Underwood Archives / agefotostock; page 18: © spatuletail / Shutterstock; page 19: © Nick Laham / Staff / Getty Images; page 19: © Gregory Shamus / Staff / Getty Images; page 20: © Jonathan Daniel / Staff / Getty Images; page 20: © Jonathan Daniel / Staff / Getty Images; page 21: © Andy Lyons / Staff / Getty Images; page 21: © Jonathan Daniel / Staff / Getty Images; page 22: © Brian Drake / SportsChrome / Newscom; page 23: © Mike Powell / Staff / Getty Images; page 23: © stevezmina1 / Getty Images; page 25: © Mike Powell / Staff / Getty Images; page 26: © File photo/TNS / Newscom; page 29: © Jonathan Daniel / Staff / Getty Images

ISBN Information
9781503857612 (Reinforced Library Binding)
9781503860438 (Portable Document Format)
9781503861794 (Online Multi-user eBook)
9781503863156 (Electronic Publication)

LCCN 2021952621

Printed in the United States of America

BRINGING THE WORLD TO YOUNG READERS 1968

TABLE OF CONTENTS

GO BEARS!

The Chicago Bears compete in the National Football **League's** (NFL) National Football Conference (NFC). They play in the NFC North **division**, along with the Green Bay Packers, Minnesota Vikings, and Detroit Lions. Fans in Chicago have been lucky! Their Bears have won more games than any other team in the entire league. The Bears also have more players in the Pro Football **Hall of Fame** than any other team. Let's learn more about the Bears!

NFC NORTH DIVISION

Chicago Bears

Detroit Lions

Green Bay Packers

Minnesota Vikings

THE NFC NORTH DIVISION CONTAINS TEAMS WITH SOME OF THE OLDEST RIVALRIES IN THE NFL. VICTORY OVER A RIVAL IS CAUSE FOR CELEBRATION.

BECOMING THE BEARS

The Bears are one of only two teams still playing who were original members of the NFL. The team began play in 1920 but was called the Decatur Staleys. They were originally named after a food company in Illinois. In 1921, team owner George Halas moved the team from Decatur to Chicago. The team played in Wrigley Field, home to baseball's Chicago Cubs. The owner said that "football players are much bigger players than baseball players, so if baseball players are cubs, then football players must be bears!" In 1922, they became the Bears!

HALL-OF-FAMER BRONISLAU 'BRONKO' NAGURSKI PLAYED FOR THE BEARS IN THE 1930S AND 1940S.

BY THE NUMBERS

EIGHT
NFL Championships for the Bears

The Bears have won **ONE** Super Bowl.

783
wins for the Bears—more than any other NFL team!

30
Bears enshrined in the Pro Football Hall of Fame

BEARS PLAYERS HAVE HAD MANY REASONS TO CELEBRATE OVER THE YEARS. THE BEARS HAVE WON MORE GAMES THAN ANY OTHER NFL TEAM!

THE PASSIONATE CROWD AT SOLDIER FIELD GIVES THE BEARS A HUGE HOME-FIELD ADVANTAGE ON GAME DAYS.

GAME DAY

The Bears play their home games in Chicago, Illinois. Their **stadium** is called Soldier Field. Soldier Field opened in 1924, but the Bears moved in for the 1971 football season. In its history, Soldier Field has hosted the soccer World Cup, the Special Olympics, and a speech by Dr. Martin Luther King Jr. The average December temperature in Chicago is between 27 and 37 degrees Fahrenheit (–2.8 and 2.8 degrees Celsius). That means fans often face freezing temperatures when they come to cheer on the Bears!

We're Famous!

A few months before winning Super Bowl 41, players on the 1985 Bears recorded a rap song called "The Super Bowl Shuffle." The song and music video became huge hits! "The Super Bowl Shuffle" appeared on the Billboard Hot 100 chart and was even nominated for a Grammy Award!

UNIFORM

Truly Weird

In 2017, the Bears played a game against the Carolina Panthers and completed only four passes. Chicago also had only five first downs during the entire game. The Panthers had possession of the ball for 17 more minutes than the Bears. But only the number on the scoreboard decides the winner of a game! The Bears had two defensive **touchdowns**, so they won the game 17–3!

Alternate Jersey

Sometimes teams wear an alternate jersey that is different from their home and away jerseys. It might be a bright color or have a unique theme. During the 2020 season, the Bears wore their orange jerseys twice. But the new look proved unlucky. The Bears lost both games.

BEARS PLAYERS RUSH ONTO THE FIELD THROUGH A GIANT INFLATABLE TUNNEL IN THE SHAPE OF A GROWLING BEAR BEFORE HOME GAMES AT SOLDIER FIELD.

TEAM SPIRIT

Cold weather doesn't stop Bears fans from having a blast at Soldier Field. Before the game even begins, a huge crowd gathers in the parking lot for a tailgating party. Fans enjoy foods like bratwurst, polish sausages, and hot dogs! One stadium tradition dates back to 1941. After every Bears touchdown, fans sing the team's fight song, "Bear Down, Chicago Bears." The Bears are one of the few NFL teams without cheerleaders. Instead, the team's mascot, Staley the Bear, entertains the crowd at every home game.

STALEY

HEROES OF HISTORY

Dick Butkus

Linebacker | 1965–1973

Known as one of the hardest hitters ever to play football, Butkus made the **Pro Bowl** eight times. He was named the NFL's Defensive Player of the Year twice. Sometimes called "The Animal," Butkus often growled before a play to intimidate opponents.

Mike Ditka

Tight End | 1961–1966

In six seasons with the Bears, Ditka gained 4,503 yards and scored 34 touchdowns. After his 12-season Hall of Fame playing career, Ditka returned to Chicago to coach the Bears. In 1985, he led the team to its only Super Bowl victory.

Matt Forte

Running Back | 2008–2015

During his eight years in Chicago, Forte averaged nearly 1,600 yards from scrimmage per season. He was equally dangerous as a pass catcher and rusher. Forte's 64 total touchdowns rank third in team history. He was chosen for the Pro Bowl twice.

Brian Urlacher

Linebacker | 2000–2012

During the 2006 season, Urlacher anchored the defense that led the Bears to Super Bowl 41. He played all 13 seasons of his career with the Bears, earning eight trips to the Pro Bowl. Urlacher ranks ninth in NFL history with 1,046 solo tackles.

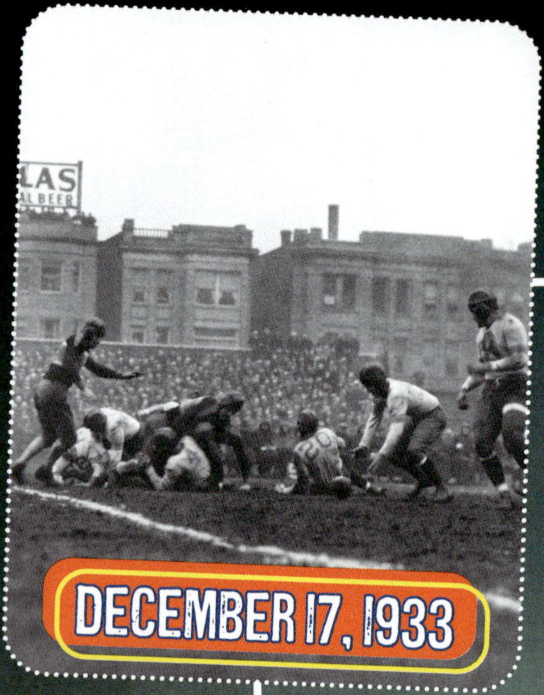

Long before the Super Bowl era, the Bears defeat the New York Giants 23–21 in the first NFL Championship Game.

Coach and team owner George Halas leads the Bears to the most lopsided victory in NFL history. They defeat Washington 73–0.

BIG DAYS

The Bears win the NFC Championship Game, defeating the New Orleans Saints 39–14. This earns the team a trip to the Super Bowl.

The Bears trade up in the NFL Draft in order to select quarterback Justin Fields with the number 11 overall selection.

MODERN-DAY MARVELS

Justin Fields

Quarterback | Debut: 2021

Fields was the Bears' first-round draft selection in 2021. The Bears made him the number 11 overall pick after a very successful college career at Ohio State University. Fields earned his first NFL victory as a starter in week four of the 2021 season when the Bears defeated the Detroit Lions 24–14.

David Montgomery

Running Back | Debut: 2019

Montgomery took control of the Bears, rushing attack right after being drafted in 2019. He is one of the more challenging backs in the league to tackle. Montgomery gained 3,732 yards from scrimmage in his first three seasons.

Al-Quadin Muhammad

Defensive End | Debut: 2022

Pictured here in his Indianapolis Colts uniform, Muhammad signed with the Bears after the 2021 season. In 2021, he started all 17 games. He finished with six sacks. He also had 32 solo tackles. Muhammad played college football for the University of Miami.

Robert Quinn

Defensive End | Debut: 2020

Quinn played for four teams before joining the Bears in 2020. He finished second in the NFL with 18.5 sacks in 2021. It was the fifth time in his career finishing with more than ten sacks. Quinn has been selected for the Pro Bowl three times.

LEGENDARY RUNNING BACK WALTER PAYTON SCORED 125 TOUCHDOWNS FOR THE BEARS.

THE GOAT

GREATEST OF ALL TIME

WALTER PAYTON

Known as "Sweetness," Walter Payton is the second-leading rusher in NFL history. He topped 1,000 yards rushing in ten different seasons and was the NFL's **Most Valuable Player** in 1977. Payton helped lead the team to their only Super Bowl victory after the 1985 season. He was inducted into the Hall of Fame in 1993. Each year, the league gives the Walter Payton NFL Man of the Year Award for a player's excellence on and off the field.

FAN FAVORITE

William Perry–Defensive Lineman

1985–1992

Known as the "Refrigerator" because of his massive size (6'2", 335 lbs.), Perry is a beloved icon in Chicago. He's had the heart of Chicago fans ever since scoring a touchdown in Super Bowl 20 during his **rookie** season. "The Fridge" even had his own G. I. Joe action figure!

THE BIG GAME

JANUARY 26, 1986 – SUPER BOWL 20

The Bears won eight NFL Championships in the pre–Super Bowl era. But after the 1985 season, the Bears finally reached the Super Bowl for the first time. The Bears held the New England Patriots without a touchdown until the fourth quarter. Popular quarterback Jim McMahon rushed for two touchdowns. Wide receiver Willie Gault caught four passes for 129 yards. Defensive end Richard Dent led Chicago's powerful defense and was named the game's Most Valuable Player. The Bears defeated the Patriots 46–10 for their first and only Super Bowl victory.

THE 1985 BEARS DEFENSE IS CONSIDERED BY SOME TO BE THE GREATEST IN NFL HISTORY.

GEORGE HALAS LED THE BEARS TO SIX NFL CHAMPIONSHIPS.

AMAZING FEATS

6 Single-Game Touchdowns

In 1965 by **RUNNING BACK** Gale Sayers

7 Forced Fumbles in a Season

In 1985 by **DEFENSIVE END** Richard Dent

1,488 Career Tackles

By **LINEBACKER** Mike Singletary

7 Single-Game Passing Touchdowns

In 1943 by **QUARTERBACK** Sid Luckman

ALL-TIME BEST

PASSING YARDS

Jay Cutler
23,443

Sid Luckman
14,686

Jim Harbaugh
11,567

RUSHING YARDS

Walter Payton
16,726

Matt Forte
8,602

Neal Anderson
6,166

RECEIVING YARDS

Johnny Morris
5,059

Harlon Hill
4,616

Alshon Jeffery
4,549

SACKS*

Richard Dent
124.5

Steven McMichael
92.5

Dan Hampton
57

SCORING

Robbie Gould
1,207

Kevin Butler
1,116

Walter Payton
750

INTERCEPTIONS

Gary Fencik
38

Richie Petitbon
37

Charles Tillman
36

*unofficial before 1982

ROBBIE GOULD CONNECTED ON MORE THAN 85 PERCENT OF HIS FIELD GOAL ATTEMPTS AS A MEMBER OF THE BEARS.

GLOSSARY

division (dih-VIZSH-un): a group of teams within the NFL who play each other more frequently and compete for the best record

Hall of Fame (HAHL of FAYM): a museum in Canton, Ohio, that honors the best players in NFL history

league (leeg): an organization of sports teams that compete against each other

Most Valuable Player (MOHST VAL-yoo-bul PLAY-uhr): a yearly award given to the top player in the NFL

Pro Bowl (PRO BOWL): the NFL's All-Star game where the best players in the league compete

rookie (RUH-kee): a player playing in his first season

sack (SAK): when a quarterback is tackled behind the line of scrimmage before he can throw the ball

stadium (STAY-dee-yum): a building with a field and seats for fans where teams play

Super Bowl (SOO-puhr BOWL): the championship game of the NFL, played between the winners of the AFC and the NFC

touchdown (TUTCH-down): a play in which the ball is brought into the other team's end zone, resulting in six points

FIND OUT MORE

IN THE LIBRARY

Bulgar, Beth and Mark Bechtel. *My First Book of Football.* New York, NY: Time Inc. Books, 2015.

Jacobs, Greg. *The Everything Kids' Football Book, 7th Edition*. Avon, MA: Adams Media, 2021.

Sports Illustrated Kids. *The Greatest Football Teams of All Time*. New York, NY: Time Inc. Books, 2018.

Wyner, Zach. *Chicago Bears*. New York, NY: AV2, 2020.

ON THE WEB

Visit our website for links about the Chicago Bears:
childsworld.com/links

Note to parents, teachers, and librarians: We routinely verify our web links to make sure they are safe and active sites. Encourage your readers to check them out!

INDEX

ABOUT THE AUTHOR

Josh Anderson has published over 50 books for children and young adults. His two boys are the greatest joys in his life. Hobbies include coaching his sons in youth basketball, no-holds-barred games of Apples to Apples, and taking long family walks. His favorite NFL team is a secret he'll never share!